D...
—FOREST—

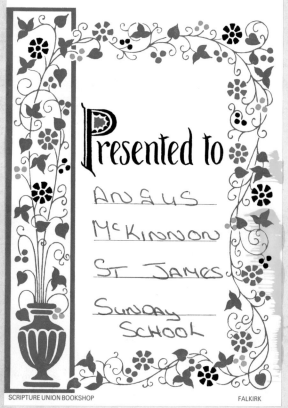

Presented to

ANGUS
MCKINNON
ST JAMES
SUNDAY
SCHOOL

the Disappearing FOREST

Peter J Dyck

Scripture Union
130 City Road, London EC1V 2NJ.

First published in the UK by Scripture Union 1992

ISBN 0 86201 787 4

Scripture quotations are from the Holy Bible, New International Version.
Copyright © 1973, 1978, 1984, International Bible Society. Published by Hodder and Stoughton

Phototypeset by Intype, London
Printed by Cox and Wyman Ltd, Reading

To our grandchildren,
Peter, Deborah, Cornelia, Sasha,
and Misha,
whose gentle pleading for
'just one more story'
sometimes works

Contents

There is no faithfulness, no love,
no acknowledgment of God in the
land . . .
Because of this the land mourns,
and all who live in it waste away;
the beasts of the field and the birds
of the air
and the fish of the sea are dying.
(Hosea 4:1–3)

They will neither harm nor destroy
on all my holy mountain,
for the earth will be full of the
knowledge of the Lord
as the waters cover the sea.
(Isaiah 11:9)

1

A Lovely Day Spoiled

Rabbit saw him first.

It was a lovely day. The sun was shining, the grass was green, and the birds were singing in the trees.

Rabbit got up from his afternoon nap. He decided this would be an excellent time to take a little hop through the woods.

He followed his usual path around the big oak trees, through the maples, and finally to the edge of the forest. He sat down under his favourite tree.

Rabbit was feeling good. For the seventeenth time that afternoon he thought how lovely the world was. Especially the forest. His little forest. Surely it was the most beautiful forest in the whole country. He was so lucky.

Rabbit was about to turn back when he heard a strange sound. It was not the kind of sound made by rabbits or his other animal friends in the forest. It was a thud kind of sound, as if something was being hit. It was a bit frightening. But Rabbit was not easily scared. He hopped forward to investigate.

From the edge of the forest he could see the town in the distance. He could see the road with cars and lorries dashing by. And he could see the farm.

Everything was as usual. Everything, except that dull and heavy thudding sound that he kept hearing. Rabbit didn't like it. He didn't know why he didn't like it, but he wished it would go away.

And then he saw him. The man with the axe. He was chopping down one of the small maples. Every time he swung his axe the sun made it shine for a brief moment while it was up in the air. Then it came down hard against the tree, shaking it from top to bottom. The birds in the branches had all flown away.

As the man kept hitting the tree with the sharp edge of the axe, Rabbit felt sick. Splinters of white wood were flying in every direction. The gash in the tree got bigger and bigger.

And then Rabbit noticed that one of the birds, Mother Blue Jay, had come back to the tree. She fluttered around the top looking for a good branch to land on.

Just then the man hit the tree again. It shook so

hard that the blue jay flew away. In a moment the brightly coloured mother was back at exactly the same spot, fluttering around nervously and making crying sounds.

Rabbit wondered what was going on. Why did she keep coming back to that spot? Why was she so nervous? Why was she calling so loudly? It sounded like a cry for help.

Rabbit didn't know that Mother Blue Jay had her nest in one of the branches at the top of that tree. He didn't know that there were three little baby blue jays in that nest.

The man finally stopped chopping and started pushing the tree over. Only then did Rabbit notice the nest. And the helpless little birds. They couldn't fly yet.

Once more Mother Blue Jay fluttered around the nest and her poor little babies. But there was nothing that she could do to save them. In the next moment the tree fell crashing to the ground with a loud thump. The earth shook. The branches quivered for a moment and then were still.

And so were the three little birds. With the fall of the tree they were thrown from their nest and hurled through the air. Like the tree, the nest and the birds were dashed to the ground. For a brief moment they, too, seemed to quiver. Then they lay still. Rabbit knew they were dead.

All this time Rabbit had been hiding under a

bush. He had watched the whole thing. He was so upset that he trembled.

And then he saw the man take a long stone out of his pocket. He stood still for a moment drawing the whetstone back and forth over the axe. He was making it sharp.

Then he wiped his forehead with a red handkerchief. He put it back in his pocket and just stood there looking at the trees. Perhaps he was deciding which one to chop down next.

Suddenly Rabbit saw the axe swinging in the air again. He saw it gleam in the sun, he heard the thud, he saw the splinters fly, and he saw all the birds fly away.

Rabbit could stand it no longer. He wasted no time hopping back into the forest to tell the other animals what he had seen. Soon Badger and Beaver, Fox and Skunk, and all the birds knew about the man cutting down the trees of their forest, destroying their homes.

They listened to Rabbit for a while. They were frightened and angry. They begged Rabbit to lead them to the man with the axe. Rabbit said he would do that if they would promise two things: to keep absolutely quiet and to keep out of sight of the man. The man must not see them or hear them.

They all promised. Actually, they didn't know what they would do when they got there. They just wanted to see for themselves this terrible thing that

Rabbit was talking about.

Rabbit led them to the edge of the forest. By that time the man had already hacked down two more small trees. While all the animals were watching him from under the bushes and behind the trees, the man suddenly stopped his chopping.

That was good. The animals were happy. They looked at each other and smiled. Rabbit was mistaken. The man was not going to cut down the whole forest. He just wanted three trees, no more.

But Rabbit was not wrong. The man carried his tools to the truck and came back with something bigger than the axe. He pulled a cord on that red thing, and suddenly it began to splutter and roar like an engine.

When the animals heard it, they were so startled that some of them jumped and others fell flat on the ground. They had no idea what it was. They were frightened.

'It's a chain-saw,' whispered Rabbit when the engine stopped for a moment. 'With that machine he can cut down trees ten times faster than with the axe.'

They watched him cut down one big tree after another. Every time a tree crashed to the ground the animals wanted to jump out of their hiding places and shout to the man: 'No! No! Please don't cut down our trees! The forest is our home! This is where we live!'

But they didn't. They remembered their promise to Rabbit. And they also knew it would do no good. The man with that sharp axe and noisy chain-saw wouldn't listen to them.

He didn't seem to care at all that the trees he had cut down were now dead. He didn't seem to care about the birds' nests that he had destroyed. He didn't seem to care even about the helpless baby birds that he had killed.

2

Move or Stay?

That night the moon filled the forest with a soft glow. When the people in the farmhouse had switched off their lights and gone to bed, all the animals and birds in the forest gathered.

They met at the same spot where the farmer had cut down the trees. Rabbit counted them. There were now more than twenty dead trees. They were stretched on the ground, some on top of each other, exactly where they had fallen. The dead baby birds were also lying where they had dropped.

From the distance came the sound of barking dogs. They were guarding the farmyard. But there was no one to guard the forest.

Finally Rabbit spoke. 'My friends,' he said, 'a

terrible thing is happening here. With your own eyes you saw the man with the axe and the chain-saw. He cut down a part of our forest. He will probably come back and cut down more trees. More of our homes will be destroyed. More baby birds will be killed.'

'That's not all,' said Badger. 'I have young ones, too. They are only four days old. We live close by here. A few more trees felled and the man will be dropping them right on top of my house and my babies.'

There was stirring and groaning among the animals. They were upset. Someone began to cry. They were frightened, and they were angry.

At last Rabbit spoke again. 'My friends and neighbours,' he said, 'does anyone have an idea what we should do?'

There was a long silence. Then Badger spoke again. 'If the man comes back and cuts down all the trees, we will be driven from our homes. Perhaps we should move now before that happens. It will be too late then.'

'No way,' shouted Fox. 'Where would we go? As you know, I leave this forest almost every night. I go exploring all over the countryside. Sometimes I find a chicken for my supper, and sometimes I don't. But I can tell you this much: I have never seen another forest like this one anywhere for miles around.'

'Fox is right,' said Beaver. 'Nobody has gone exploring as far as our friend Fox has. If he says there isn't another forest to move to, I believe him. As far as I am concerned, that settles it. We stay right here!'

Rabbit cleared his throat and asked what the other animals and birds thought. 'What do the rest of you say? Do we move or do we stay?'

They all shouted: 'No move! We stay!'

Again there followed a long silence. Mother Blue Jay and some of her cousins were standing around their dead baby birds. They had stopped crying but were very sad.

Some clouds drifted silently past the full moon and floated a shadow across the animals. They were all thinking. At last Rabbit spoke again.

'Okay! Then it is agreed that we stay. But you all know what that means. It means that we have to stop the man from cutting down our forest. We have to stop him from destroying our homes.'

'And killing our babies,' sighed Mother Blue Jay sadly as she stepped away from her dead children to join the circle.

There was more silence. And then Rabbit said: 'What we need is a plan. We have to think of things we can do to stop the man with that axe and horrible chain-saw. We need a strategy.'

Badger didn't know what a strategy was, so Fox quietly explained it to him. 'Strategy is a plan of action,' he whispered, 'a carefully worked-out method for defeating an enemy.'

They all talked about this for a while but got nowhere. Rabbit couldn't get them thinking about strategy because some of them still thought the man would stop by himself.

But the next day the man was back again. This time he hadn't just come with the axe and the chain-saw; he had brought his tractor. All the animals watched him from their hiding places as he sawed the largest branches from the trees which he had cut down the day before.

Then he hooked a huge logging chain to the tractor and dragged out the logs, branches, and trees lying on the ground. All morning the tractor roared as the man drove back and forth pulling trees out of the forest. It was so noisy that the animals couldn't even hear each other when they spoke.

At last the man was finished. The animals waited to see what he would do next.

Badger thought he might go home and not cut down any more. That would solve their problem.

Beaver thought he might just chop down a few more and then stop. That would give him enough firewood for heating his house in the winter.

None of the animals was prepared for what they saw next.

The man tied one end of a long chain to his tractor

and the other end around a small tree. Then he climbed onto his tractor and opened the hand throttle. The tractor roared, the chain became taut, the tree shook and bent – but it didn't fall over.

The man wanted to pull the trees out with the tractor, instead of using the axe and the chain-saw to cut them down. For a moment it looked as if his plan wouldn't work.

Fox saw the tractor back up and heard its engine idling. For half a minute the man sat quietly on his seat wiping his hot face with the red handkerchief. Fox was just getting ready to whisper a happy 'hurrah' to Badger behind the next bush.

Then the animals saw how he put the throttle wide open and popped the clutch out. The tractor howled and lurched forward with a jerk.

Before the animals could blink twice, the tree was on its side, the roots pulled out of the ground, and off they went – the man, the tractor, and the tree. He towed it over to the growing pile of the other dead trees.

By the time the sun set in the evening, the man had uprooted and dragged out more than thirty trees.

3

Planning Strategy

That night the animals and birds met again. They were so upset that they all talked at the same time. At last Rabbit asked them to be quiet and pay attention.

'Now it is quite clear,' he said. 'The man is not just cutting down a few trees for firewood. He is not just getting a little wood to build something with. He is going to cut down the whole forest. He probably sold this land to a developer who wants to turn our forest into a car-park.'

'Or into a factory to make weapons,' added Beaver. 'You know how humans kill each other with guns and bombs.'

'And factories produce a lot of poison,' said

Badger. 'Factories pollute the air and the water with their waste products.'

'That's right,' agreed Beaver. 'And when they have finished making their terrible weapons, they have so much toxic waste material left over. The only way they know how to get rid of it is to dig a big hole in the ground and bury it. But after a while the poison seeps out and spoils the land.'

Rabbit summed up the view of the animals and birds: 'It's very frightening, whatever it is that the man plans to do with this forest. Whether he plans to turn it into a car-park or a polluting factory, we don't know. What we do know is that soon we will have no forest at all.

'We agreed to stop him. The question is how? This is our strategy meeting. Tonight we must make plans to save our forest-home. If anyone has an idea how we can do that, please speak up.'

'I say, let's call the wolf,' said someone from the back in an angry voice. 'He can tear the man to pieces!'

'Did you say wolf?' asked Rabbit in surprise. 'I'm sure you didn't mean that.'

'Yes, I did,' snarled the same voice from the back. 'Why not? How else are you going to stop him? I say, let's call the wolf. Why isn't he at this meeting anyway? Let's kill the man!'

There followed an awkward silence. At last Rabbit spoke. His voice was clear and carried a tone of authority. 'In the first place, the wolf probably wouldn't do it. Wolves don't attack people just like that,' he explained.

'In the second place, that's really not our way of solving problems. We believe killing the man would not make a safe life for us at all. It would create new and bigger problems. All we want is for him to stop cutting down our beautiful forest and destroying our homes.'

Everyone agreed that Rabbit had spoken well. Badger said, 'Let's not kill the man. Let's just stop him!'

The birds had been quiet at the first meeting. Now Starling reported that they had been having a meeting of their own. They had hatched a plan.

Beaver wanted to laugh and say that birds ought to be hatching eggs, not plans, but he knew they wouldn't think that was funny. Everybody was serious, so he said nothing.

'What plan did you birds hatch?' asked Rabbit. 'Please tell us about it.'

'We are not strong like the man and his tractor,' Starling began. 'But we are many, and the man is only one. We can fly, and the man cannot. So we do have some advantages over him.

'We thought that perhaps we could fly above him and around him really fast and scarylike. At the same time we would make as much noise as possible.

'Some of us are good at diving. We could just

drop out of the sky like an arrow and pretend we're going straight for the man. Perhaps that would drive him away.'

Beaver was just about to laugh and say the birds needed to hatch a better plan than that. But Rabbit spoke first.

'That's good. Your plan may not be the best, but it's worth a try. I like the idea that you birds are thinking of joining us animals in the fight to save our forest. That is great. Keep thinking and keep chirping. You are hatching a good plan. By the way, do you have a label for your strategy, a code name for your plan?'

'Yes, we do,' replied Starling. 'We thought of calling it Operation Feathers.'

'Operation Feathers sounds interesting,' said Rabbit. 'A bit soft and fluffy, but why not? I like it!'

Badger said he also had an idea. There were many things that he could not do, he admitted. Smiling kindly at Starling, he acknowledged that he couldn't fly.

But there was one thing that he could do well. So well that he was an expert at it. He even spent most of his life doing it.

'What is it? Tell us,' asked Rabbit. 'Don't keep us waiting. What is it that you do so well?'

'The one thing I do best is dig,' answered Badger. 'Look at my paws. Look at my legs. You can see that they are made for digging. I dig tunnels under the ground. As you all know. I dug my own house under the ground.'

'Yes, yes,' said Rabbit excitedly, 'but what has that to do with stopping the man from destroying our forest? Please tell us. We're waiting to hear it.'

'Tell us! Tell us now!' shouted someone impatiently from the back.

'My plan is to upset the man's tractor,' replied Badger. 'If you want me to, I could lay that farmer's tractor on its side as if it were sleeping.'

'How are you going to do that? All of us together couldn't lift that tractor off the ground an inch,' said Beaver. 'And you talk about upsetting it all by yourself?'

'Simple,' replied Badger, 'really easy. Remember, I'm a digger, an earthmover. I plan to dig away the earth under one side of the tractor to make a trench, a large hole. When I'm done the tractor will simply fall over into the hole all by itself.'

'That's a splendid idea!' cried Rabbit. And all the animals agreed. Somebody said that when the tractor would fall into the hole, it would be like falling into its grave. Everybody clapped their hands. 'Badger the gravedigger,' someone shouted happily.

'Have you given your strategy a name, too?' asked Rabbit.

'Yes, I have,' replied Badger. 'If it's all right with

you and the others, I'd like to call it Operation Topple.'

'Magnificent!' said Rabbit. 'Operation Topple is a good code name for a great idea. Are there any more schemes? Please speak up. We need all the help we can get.'

4

More Schemes

'Badger has just given me an idea,' said Beaver. 'There is one thing that I also can do better than anything else. No, I can't fly like Starling and I can't dig like Brother Badger. But I make things happen with water.

'As you all know, my family and I live in the lake in the centre of the woods. But what you probably don't know is that at one time there was no lake here at all. There was just a little stream flowing into the forest at one end and out at the other.

'My grandfather was the first to think of building a dam across the stream to stop the water from flowing away. He started to build the dam, and soon there was a little pond.

'My father and mother kept on building it and turned the pond into a lake. My wife and I and even our children have made the dam still taller and stronger. Today it holds back all the water that you see in the lake. Our beaver house is actually inside the dam.'

At last Beaver stopped talking. Everyone had listened attentively. Most of the animals had no notion that the beavers had actually made that lake themselves. All they knew was that the lake provided water for them to drink and splash around in.

They couldn't imagine doing without that lake. Nor could they imagine what Beaver had in mind when he said, 'I can make things happen with water.'

Rabbit cleared his throat and said: 'Beaver, we didn't know that you and your family had made that lake. All of us enjoy it and benefit from it. We want to thank you for it.'

Beaver bowed his head slightly and said they were happy to share it. But he didn't want to give the wrong impression and have the animals think they had made the lake for them.

'We made the lake for ourselves,' he confessed quite honestly. 'But we certainly are happy to share it with the rest of you, with the fish, and even the birds.'

'No problem with that,' responded Rabbit. 'But

how the lake came to be is only half the story, I suppose.'

'Please tell us, Brother Beaver: what do you have in mind? How do you plan to help us stop the man from destroying our forest? What exactly has the lake to do with that? What did you mean when you said that you can make things happen with water?'

'Look at my teeth,' replied Beaver. 'Badger showed you his claws and said they were made for digging. Now I am showing you my teeth because they are made for biting.'

Everyone looked at Beaver's sharp teeth. Several animals said 'Oh my' and 'I didn't know that!'

Beaver continued. 'The thing we beavers bite best is wood. That dam holding back the water in the lake is made out of wood. Many trees and branches are stuck together with mud.

'My plan is that my family and I do in reverse what my parents and grandparents have done when they built the dam – we will break it open!'

There were groans and sighs in the audience. Somebody said, 'Oh no!' Another voice said, 'That's asking too much!'

Then Rabbit spoke. 'Brother Beaver, we do appreciate your help. But tell us more about your plan to save our forest. Tell us how cutting the dam will stop the man from destroying the forest. It seems to me there is too much destruction already.'

'Yes and no,' replied Beaver. 'My plan is quite

simple. When we breach the dam, the water will rush out and flood the land. Then it will be impossible for the man and his tractor to come here to tear out more trees.'

Everyone agreed that it was the noblest thing anyone could do to give up his lake and house to save the forest. Again Beaver bowed his head slightly and said it was the only thing he could do. And, he assured them, he would immediately start building another dam and making a new lake as soon as the farmer had stopped cutting down the forest.

'We have three ideas so far,' said Rabbit. 'The birds plan to stop the man by flying over and around him until he gets so nervous that he gives up and goes home. Badger plans to dig a hole beside the tractor to make it fall into its grave. Beaver has volunteered to break the dam and flood the land so the woodcutter can't come near the forest.

'We have Operation Feathers and Operation Topple. Are there any other ideas? This is a good strategy meeting. Your ideas and plans are excellent. By the way, Beaver, what is the code name for your plan?'

'Operation Water,' replied Beaver. Everybody liked that, and some repeated to themselves, 'Operation Water.'

For a while it looked as if there might be no more ideas. Then a thin, little voice spoke up and said she had an idea. Everybody looked around but couldn't see who was speaking.

Rabbit asked, 'Where are you?'

The little voice replied, 'Here I am.' Still nobody could see who was speaking.

'Please tell us who you are,' asked Rabbit politely. 'We want to hear what you have to say.'

'I am Madam Mosquito,' said the little voice, 'and I am right here in the grass. All my brothers and sisters, some cousins, and their cousins are here with me.

'All of you have a thing that you can do better than anyone else. We lady mosquitoes also have one thing that is our speciality. We can sting like a needle. Our plan is that when the woodcutter comes back again, we zoom right up to him and sting him all over his body. That will drive him away.'

'Just a moment, please,' said Rabbit. 'Several of the animals and birds want to say something to me. Perhaps they have a question.'

Rabbit leaned over to Badger and Beaver, who motioned him to come closer. They whispered something into his ear.

Then Rabbit spoke again: 'If Madam Mosquito will please excuse us for another few minutes we need to discuss something among ourselves.'

All the animals huddled together off to one side and lowered their voices so that Mosquito couldn't hear them. Badger spoke first. 'The mosquitoes are not our friends,' he said. 'I don't think they should be allowed to join us.'

'What do you say, Brother Beaver?' asked Rabbit.

'I say mosquitoes have stung me a lot. I don't particularly like them nor the idea of them fighting with us. We don't need them. We can do it alone, without their help. Thank you.'

'And you,' asked Rabbit, turning to the birds, 'what do you say?'

'We feel just a bit different about it,' replied Starling.

'Of course you would,' snapped Beaver, and was a bit surprised at the harsh tone of his own voice. 'The mosquitoes never sting you the way they sting us.'

'Maybe so,' answered Starling good-naturedly because she didn't want to start a quarrel. This was no time for the animals and birds to start fighting among themselves. They needed to be united against their common enemy, the woodcutter. So Starling began once more.

'The way we birds see it, we can use all the help we can get. The mosquitoes provide lunch for some of us birds. They are not exactly our friends, but if they will be on our side it would be a help. And you animals know best how much they can sting.'

'That's right,' said Rabbit. 'We certainly do. They're no fun to have around. Do you have something more to say?'

'Yes, we do,' answered Starling. 'We think this would be a good chance to kill two birds with one stone.' Everybody laughed when Starling talked like that. They knew that she was pretending to talk like people.

'What I have in mind is that we let the mosquitoes help us drive the man away. For letting them join us, we make them promise not to sting any animals in the forest for at least one year.'

'Now that *is* killing two birds with one stone,' replied Rabbit. 'It's a marvellous idea. What do you say, Beaver and Badger? What's your reaction, Skunky?'

They all agreed to the plan and said the mosquitoes could join them. But only if they promised not to sting them for a whole year.

When Rabbit told Madam Mosquito what they had decided, it was clear that she didn't like it. 'We need blood,' said Madam Mosquito, 'just like you, Rabbit, need grass and carrots.

'How are we going to stay healthy if we can't suck a little drop of blood out of you animals every now and then? We are sorry it hurts a bit, but we can't help that. You must not think that we sting you for the fun of it, or because we are angry. We really do like you all, more perhaps than you realise. But we can't suck blood without stinging.'

Then all the mosquitoes went off into a huddle

to one side and lowered their voices. The animals couldn't hear their discussion. At last they came back and Madam Mosquito announced:

'It's a deal. We don't like your condition, but we accept it. We won't suck blood out of any of you for one year. But when that man comes, you just watch us get into action.

'Our plan is to start on his face and hands first. Then some of us will get down into his neck. At the same time others will crawl up his trouser legs and sting him there. We have a plan to sting the man at least 170 times in the first attack and 280 times in the second attack.

'He will swat some of us, but we are prepared to die for the cause. The good cause of saving the forest.'

'Bravo, bravo!' shouted Rabbit. 'Well spoken! That is a marvellous plan. That's real strategy. I'd say that's really attacking the man where it is going to hurt. And do you also have a code name for your plan?'

'We would like to call it Operation Sting,' replied Mosquito.

'Wonderful!' replied Rabbit. 'I like that. Operation Sting should be quite effective.'

5

Topple and Sting

Two days later the animals, birds, and mosquitoes were ready to carry out their plans. They didn't want to do it the day after the strategy meeting because Badger wanted to sharpen his claws some more. Beaver wanted to enjoy one more quiet day in his home in the dam before tearing it apart.

The mosquitoes said they needed to practise stinging and crawling under people's clothing. The birds also wanted to practise diving in the air and screeching to make sure the timing was right. They thought it best to follow immediately after the mosquitoes had done their sting attack.

At last they felt they were ready. The plan was clear. The strategy had been carefully worked out.

Rabbit went through it step by step for the last time.

Badger was to be first with Operation Topple. He would work during the night. By morning he would have the hole dug and the tractor toppled into it.

Then when the man came to the woods the mosquitoes would attack until they were played out. Next the birds would do their skydiving and screeching until the man couldn't take it any more.

Then Beaver and his family would open the dam and let the lake flood all the land as far as the farm and the village. Everybody knew what to do and when to do it.

The next morning the man was back bright and early, pulling out trees with his tractor. There was no mistake about it; he intended to rip out the whole forest. Maybe he wanted to turn it into a car-park, or a factory, or a cornfield. The animals and birds paid no attention to him. They didn't even watch him.

They were too busy with their own plans. They knew one thing that the man on his roaring, stinking, and smoke-belching tractor didn't know. They knew that this was the last day that he would be uprooting trees and destroying the forest.

The following morning when the sun rose, there wasn't a cloud in the sky. A gentle breeze moved the treetops, swaying them back and forth like a baby's cradle.

Outwardly everything seemed peaceful and quiet. However, under the bushes, behind the trees, and in the grass there was a lot of activity. The forest had never been more alive than on this morning. Each animal was prepared.

Again, Rabbit saw the man first. He was walking toward the tractor. Rabbit watched the expression on his face when he saw the tractor lying on its side in a big hole. Badger had done his work well.

For a moment the man just stood there beside the toppled tractor. He probably couldn't believe what his eyes saw. How could this have happened? Where did that huge hole in the ground come from all of a sudden? How would he ever get his tractor righted and out of that hole?

The man looked here and there. He circled the hole like someone walking on the edge of an open grave. He stopped and muttered some awful words that Rabbit couldn't understand. Then he stamped his feet on the ground several times. Rabbit could see that the man was upset and angry.

So far, so good, thought Rabbit. And now it was time for phase two of the strategy to begin. He looked for the mosquitoes. Before he could give them their signal to attack, the man turned and walked away. He went back to the farm buildings. But he walked so fast he almost ran.

'Let him go,' shouted Rabbit to the mosquitoes, who were just then ready to attack. 'Let's see what he's going to do next.'

They didn't have to wait long. The man had hardly reached the farm when they saw him coming back with his big truck. He backed the truck around to the toppled tractor. Then he tied the truck and tractor together with a thick chain. He climbed back into the cab of the truck.

It was clear that he was trying to pull the tractor upright with his truck. The only thing wrong was that it didn't work. The tractor was too heavy and the truck was not strong enough. The wheels began spinning in the soft soil as if they were on ice. He tried several times, but it was no use.

All this time millions of mosquitoes had been hiding in the grass around the truck and the tractor. They were ready to do their stinging, but waited for the signal from Rabbit to start. Rabbit was the overall commander, and Madame Mosquito was in charge of this operation.

The man got out of the truck and walked to the back of it. He took another look at the toppled tractor.

And then they heard Rabbit. Not loud and not at all angry, as some had expected. They simply heard him say: 'Now! Go for it!'

Rabbit wished all the animals and birds could have seen what he saw next. Suddenly the air was full of mosquitoes, like a cloud! And since they had practised their flight plans the day before, they all knew exactly what to do. Not a second was wasted.

Some went straight for the man's face. Others attacked his hands and arms. Still others were crawling down his neck and up his trouser legs to the softer skin.

The man started to thrash his arms about like a windmill. It looked as if he had suddenly gone wild. He swatted his face and slapped his hands.

When he started to jump up and down, Rabbit knew that the leg-fellows had arrived and were doing their thing. When some mosquitoes were killed or got tired, others immediately slipped in and took their place.

Suddenly the man could stand it no longer. He dashed back into the truck and slammed the door behind him. He sat there for a while before he realised what actually had happened. He was trapped!

He couldn't drive away in the truck because it was tied to the tractor. And he couldn't go out because then the mosquitoes would get him.

The mosquitoes wanted to make sure the man understood that they meant business. They were not simply fooling around or having a bit of fun with him.

Thousands and millions of them landed on the windscreen and the windows. For a moment it looked from the inside as if someone had drawn blinds over them. The man couldn't see a thing. All he saw was a wall of mosquitoes draped over his windows.

The man was not the only one pondering what to do next. Madam Mosquito, who was in charge of Operation Sting, also wondered what they should do next. She didn't have to wait long. Presently she heard Rabbit in his firm, calm, and clear voice:

'Back off! Operation Sting is interrupted. Do you hear me? Only interrupted, not finished. Everybody disappear.'

Just like that the air was instantly clear. One could see not a single mosquito anywhere. Slowly the man opened the truck door. He waited. Then he crawled out. Rabbit could tell he didn't trust the situation. He kept the door open so he could jump back in again in case the mosquitoes returned.

They didn't come back. They stayed in the grass where nobody could see them. The man quickly unhitched the truck from the tractor. He dropped the heavy chain and scrambled back into the truck. In a flash he and his truck disappeared, trailing a cloud of dust behind them. And leaving the tractor on its side exactly the way Badger had toppled it.

'Well done! Splendid, absolutely splendid!' shouted Rabbit as he jumped out from behind the bush where he had been hiding and watching the whole operation.

'Now we wait for the man's next move before we decide what to do. Meanwhile, everybody relax and get yourself something to eat. Then wait for my command.

'It's just possible that the birds may be next, but I don't know. Depends on the man. Maybe I'll call on you mosquitoes again for phase two of Operation Sting.'

6

Operation Stink

For several hours nothing happened. There was peace in the forest. Rabbit could hear the dog barking on the farm. Then he heard loud voices. He heard another tractor start. And then he saw the man coming back. This time he was coming with a tractor three times as powerful as the truck.

Rabbit had a quick word with Madam Mosquito. He thought it would be best to hold off the birds and try phase two of Operation Sting. Both agreed that the first attack had been surprisingly effective. Rabbit was quick to praise Madam Mosquito for her excellent work.

They agreed that a repeat performance would be good strategy. That way the man would know the mosquitoes weren't just after a little drop of blood. They were after *him*. They wanted him to understand their purpose. They wouldn't leave him alone until he gave up his mad plan of destroying the forest.

However, no sooner had the man returned with the monster tractor than a new situation arose. Like the first time, the mosquitoes went for him, but fell back before they actually attacked. It looked as if they had flown into a brick wall.

Rabbit couldn't understand it. They had been so bold and brave before. Why didn't they attack now? And why were they all coughing and spluttering? Why were they rubbing their noses as if they wanted to wipe something off?

With three quick hops he was beside Madam Mosquito. 'What's the matter?' he asked. 'Why aren't they attacking?'

'Rabbit,' she said, 'the man has sprayed himself with some horrible mosquito repellent stuff. We can't take that. It doesn't kill us, but as soon as we breathe it into our lungs we become almost paralysed. There's nothing we can do against it.

'We can't get close to the man. And just look at those mosquitoes over there. They're all vomiting. It's awful!'

For a moment Rabbit was deep in thought, rubbing his whiskers, and saying to himself, 'So that's it! Mosquito repellent lotion. Well, what next?'

And then a smile came over his face. The smile grew wider and bigger. Rabbit had an idea.

'Did you say it stinks?' he asked Madam Mosquito.

'Yes, it stinks. Worse than the rottenest stuff you ever smelled in your life,' she replied.

'Good, good,' said Rabbit. 'Let's change our strategy. Let's fight fire with fire! Ha, ha, ha! Let's fight stink with stink!'

Hopping off to the side he called out, 'Skunky, where are you? Come here at once. We've got the perfect job for you.'

As Skunk approached, Rabbit was rubbing his paws with glee and jumping around for joy. 'Skunky, my friend,' he began, 'I want you to sneak over to the man without him noticing you. Get right under the tractor.

'Hold your juice for that one big squirt when you can douse the man from top to bottom. Is that clear?

'Don't waste your precious perfume by spraying it on the tractor or into the air. Get it onto the man. Soak his clothes and everything. Get it into his hair. By the way, Skunky, how far can you squirt?'

'Depends on the wind,' replied Skunk. 'If there's no wind I can squirt several feet, maybe a yard or two. But if I have to squirt against the wind, it's not much use.'

'Well, then squirt with the wind,' said Rabbit. 'Get to the other side of him so the wind will carry your spray. Is your bag full now? Are you ready?'

Skunk told Rabbit that his bag was so full that if he'd run in another drop it would spill over. Yes, he was ready.

Slowly and carefully he crept out of the bushes. When the man turned away, he dashed quickly across the open space and got safely to the tractor. So far so good. But there was no way he could reach the man from there. It was too far.

Skunk was in a tight spot. How could he get within a few feet of the man, especially since he had to back up to him? His squirt gun was in his rear end.

Even if he would just run up to the man and take him by surprise, what good would that do? Before he could spray him he would have to come to a complete stop, turn around, and only then would he be ready to squirt.

By that time the man would probably either have run away or banged a shovel over his head. The man might knock him out. He could also kill him with that big chain he was holding in his hand.

For a moment Skunk wasn't sure he wanted to go through with Operation Stink, which is what Rabbit called it. What if he got hurt? Or even killed? And he really hadn't volunteered for such hazardous duty anyhow.

But then he realised that having come this far, there was probably no way to get out of completing the job. Squatting low under the tractor, he could see Rabbit near the bush. Rabbit was making signs and waving him on.

Just then the man came back to the monster tractor. He climbed up the three steps and went into the cab. That was Skunk's chance. Quickly he slipped over to the fallen tractor and let himself down into the hole.

Rabbit couldn't see him any more. He knew that Skunk was hiding somewhere in the hole, beside or under the toppled tractor.

The man came out of the cab. In his hand he carried a pair of gloves. He went down three steps, put his gloves on, and picked up one end of the chain. He pulled the chain after him right over to the hole where the fallen tractor lay.

Rabbit knew that he was going to fasten the two ends of the chain to the two tractors. Just like he had done before with the truck. Now he was going to use the monster tractor to pull the other tractor out of its grave.

To fasten the chain to the tractor on its side, he had to climb right into the hole. Rabbit watched him slide over the edge. His heart beat wildly as he thought how close the man must now be to Skunky. The question was, who would see whom first?

Would Skunk see the man first or would the man

see the skunk first? If the man saw Skunk first, he'd probably bash his brains out with that chain. And that would be the end of it. Poor Skunky wouldn't have a chance to turn around and do his squirting.

Rabbit was straining his eyes to see what was happening. He was listening intently for any sound coming from the hole. There was nothing. He couldn't see anything nor hear anything. The suspense was almost too much for Rabbit.

Suddenly he heard a loud shriek. The next moment he saw the man popping out of the hole as if he had been shot up by a cannon. In the same moment he saw Skunky leaving the hole and streaking for cover in the forest. Rabbit knew that Operation Stink had been successful.

The man was running around in circles. He was tearing at his jacket and shirt. Finally he got them both off and threw them on the ground. He acted like a man on fire. He ran his fingers through his hair again and again. He wiped his face with his red handkerchief. He looked like a man who was at the end of his wits.

Once more he left the toppled tractor exactly where Badger had dropped it and drove away.

7

Friend or Enemy?

Moments later Rabbit, Badger, Beaver, Skunk, Starling, and the mosquitoes gathered around the toppled tractor. They wanted to hug Skunk but didn't. Just in case he had a few drops of his perfume left in his bag.

'So far so good!' shouted Rabbit, delighted. 'That was a great performance, Skunky. We all thank you. I wonder what the man's wife will say when he brings that stink into the house. She will probably burn his clothes. But how will they get rid of the smell in his hair?'

Rabbit paused a bit and then continued: 'Ah, well! That's his problem. The important question is, will he now leave us alone? And if not, what will he do next?'

Madam Mosquito said that if he had anti-mosquito lotion he probably also had something to fight off skunks and badgers. They all agreed that the situation was serious, that the battle was not yet over. Whatever happened, they must act together to save their forest.

And then Rabbit said something he had never said so clearly before. Something that almost broke up the unity and started the animals and birds fighting among themselves. Rabbit said that he hoped that when it was all over, the man would be their friend. That did it!

'He is our enemy now,' said Badger, 'and he will always be our enemy. There is no way we creatures of the forest can be a friend with a human.' Several voices shouted, 'Hear, hear!' There was general applause.

'Rabbit, you surprise me,' said Beaver. 'You know what the man has done to us and plans to continue doing to us. Yet you talk about having him for a friend. Can you have someone for a friend who willfully destroys your home? Someone who deliberately wrecks your entire neighbourhood?'

'And kills your innocent babies?' added Starling.

Rabbit seemed outnumbered. But he was not ready to give in. When Skunk asked him to explain himself, he scratched his head, sat down, and motioned for the others to sit with him.

'It's like this,' Rabbit began. 'You say we should hate the man. I agree that what he is doing is terrible. We must stop him. You say that he is our enemy. Well, so he is. But if the only way we can stop him is to hate him, it seems to me we will end up hating not only him but also each other and even ourselves.'

Rabbit could see the bewildered look on their faces. He knew they didn't understand. So he continued. 'Hate is like that. Once you start hating you can't stop. Before you know it your whole life is filled with hate.

'If we can't be friends with the man once we have the victory, but go on hating him, it will be like poison in our system. I'm afraid it will slowly kill all of us. The joy and fun will go out of our life.'

Again he paused. Then he added, 'You know how it was when the snake was with us.'

When Rabbit mentioned the snake, they all started talking at once. Everybody had something to say even if no one was listening. Skunk had had little to do with the snake and hardly remembered what exactly had happened. Someone said that they surely didn't want to go through anything like that again. Everybody agreed.

'Then you understand,' said Rabbit. 'Now the man is destroying our forest. But if we start hating, then hate will destroy us!'

There was a long pause. Nobody spoke. Some animals were nodding to Rabbit, indicating that he was right. The birds thought that what he had said made a lot of sense.

At last Rabbit spoke again. 'Thank you. You are so wonderful. I'm proud of each one of you. In this meeting it has become clear to me that we have not one but two jobs to do.

'The first job is to stop the man from ripping out our forest. The second job is to win him back as our friend. And I don't know which of the two is going to be more difficult.'

They were sitting around in their friendly circle, happy that their problem had been cleared up. Then they heard the roar of the monster tractor.

Starling volunteered to fly quickly and find out what was going on. Within minutes she was back. The news was not good. She said the man was coming with a gun and some huge steel traps.

Quickly Rabbit commanded: 'Down everybody. Let's keep low so he won't see us. We must think fast. And keep our eyes open. We've got to figure out our next move.'

'Do you want us to open the dam and flood the land?' asked Beaver. 'Shall we start Operation Water?'

Most of them thought it was too early for that. The flooding should be the last thing that they would do.

The mosquitoes said they were ready for phase two of Operation Sting, but just then Madam Mosquito landed with a bit of a bump near Rabbit and said she had already flown out to the man to investigate. He had even more mosquito repellent stuff on him than before. No way could the mosquitoes attack.

'That settles it,' said Rabbit. 'It's time for the birds. Time for the skydiving and screeching to begin. Madam Starling, are you ready to start Operation Feathers?'

'Yes,' said Madam Starling, 'we are ready. Operation Feathers may sound soft, but it's going to be hard on the man's backbone. We'll shatter his nerves!'

'Good,' replied Rabbit. 'I'll watch the man and you watch me. When I thump three times with my left foot, that's your signal to start the attack.'

8

Traps and Snares

Meanwhile, the man was coming nearer and nearer to the forest. Rabbit wanted him to come as close as possible before giving the signal for the attack.

This would give the birds a chance to fly back into the forest in case of trouble. He didn't think it would be wise to attack out in the open field where the birds had no cover.

And it was a good thing that Rabbit planned it that way. As soon as he thumped three times and the birds began their attack, the man reached for his gun and started shooting. Operation Feathers had only begun and already there were five dead birds and at least eleven that were wounded.

'This is terrible,' said Madam Starling. 'He's

killing us. What shall we do?'

'Stop the attack!' shouted Rabbit. 'Stop Operation Feathers at once!'

Instantly the birds disappeared into the tree-tops and deeper into the forest. And just in time, too. By now the man was shooting like mad. He had killed a few more birds since the first count. One of them was the sister of Madam Starling. They had both hatched in the same nest. Not only had he shot her dead, but when she fell to the ground the tractor ran over her.

When Operation Feathers stopped, the man grabbed the steel traps and disappeared with them into the forest. He didn't stay long, and nobody could see what he did with them.

When he came back to his monster tractor, he didn't have the traps with him. Rabbit knew that he had set them somewhere for the animals in the forest.

As soon as the man was gone, everybody crowded around Rabbit. Obviously things were getting out of hand. Operation Feathers had been a disaster.

And what about the traps? What if somebody accidentally stepped onto one of those traps? And what should be the next move in case the man came back? Would this be the time for Operation Water?

They were still discussing all this when they saw the monster tractor coming back.

'Down everybody,' whispered Rabbit. 'Let's

keep our eyes open and meet again as soon as he's gone.'

To the surprise of everyone the man pulled something from his tractor that they could not identify. They had never seen anything like that before. They hadn't the faintest idea what it was used for. It looked like a lot of string tangled and perhaps tied together.

The man carried it to the trees. He had both arms full, holding it the way one might carry an armful of grass or hay. Some of it slipped down, and he stepped on it, which almost tripped him.

At last he threw the whole heap on the ground and began to untangle it. It took him a long time, and he tied parts of it to different trees. Then he left, and the animals relaxed.

'Glad he's gone,' said Rabbit, when they all got together again. 'And glad that this time he didn't come with another trick to hurt us. Does anybody know what that thing is that he tied to the trees?'

None of the animals knew. Badger thought it was probably for catching leaves. All agreed that it was harmless.

'Harmless!' snapped Madam Starling, 'Harmless, is it? For catching leaves, is it? Well, let me tell you, it's not harmless, and it's not for catching leaves. It's for catching us. It's a snare for birds! It's as dangerous for us as the steel traps are for you.'

'Snare!' the animals repeated. 'A snare to catch

birds with! How awful! How absolutely dreadful! What are you going to do about it?'

'For one thing,' replied Starling, 'let all the birds know about it at once. And for another, try to keep the young ones away from it. The little ones are always so curious, but once they're in that net they'll never get out. They're trapped.'

Just then there was a piercing scream from the forest that made the animals and birds look around as if to ask, 'What was that?' They could see fear in each other's eyes.

'My wife!' cried Beaver. 'That sounded like my wife.' He dashed off into the forest in the direction of the scream. All the animals followed him.

Moments later they found Betty Beaver, crying for help and unable to move. 'What is it?' asked Beaver. 'What happened?'

'It's my leg,' she said. 'It hurts and I can't move it.' They pushed some loose twigs and leaves aside and found a steel trap hidden underneath. She hadn't seen it because it was covered. She had stepped on it, and it had snapped shut around her leg.

'Hold still, dear,' said Beaver. 'We'll get you out of this in no time. Badger, Rabbit, and Fox, will you please give me a hand with this trap so we can set my wife free?'

They tried. They worked most of the afternoon. They could not open the trap. Meanwhile, the leg was bleeding so badly that the grass and the whole area around poor Betty was red with blood. Just when they thought of one more try, Betty fainted.

Everybody was shaken. They were afraid. And now they were also tired from trying to free Mrs. Beaver. Things were not going well for the animals, nor for the birds either.

Sitting around the unconscious Betty Beaver for a little rest, nobody knew what to do next. They all looked at their natural leader, Rabbit. He sat there as sad and silent as the rest of them. At last Fox spoke up.

'This is not good,' he said, 'but it could be worse. A lot worse. You all know what I mean. Think about what happens next. The man will come back with his gun, take aim, and shoot Betty Beaver dead. That would be worse.

'That's not happened yet. But that's why he set the trap to catch her. And others. He wants to kill all of us. And trapping us first is just his way of making it easier for himself.'

Everyone listened attentively, and some nodded their heads. But so far Fox, who had the reputation of being clever, hadn't really said anything that the others didn't already know.

'Okay. So what?' asked Rabbit a bit impatiently. 'We all agree with what you have said. But the real question is, how do we get poor Betty Beaver out of this trap? We need an immediate answer.'

'I was just coming to that,' replied Fox. 'The reason I am so slow is because what I am going to propose is . . . just a bit shocking. Some of you will think it's cruel. Some of you may even accuse me of not having any feelings at all. And then again . . .'

'Out with it!' snapped Rabbit. 'Say it! Betty is bleeding to death, and we sit around and talk. At least now she doesn't feel the pain. But any moment she'll regain consciousness and feel the hurt again.'

'That's right,' replied Brother Beaver. 'And any moment now the man might come back with his gun and . . .'

'Hold it, hold it right there!' cried Fox. 'I'll tell you what I have in mind. It's been done before. Once when my uncle Willie . . .'

'Fox,' yelled Rabbit louder than he had intended to. 'Fox, if you have anything to say, if you have any idea how to save Betty's life, then say it now. Or hold your peace.'

'Bite off her leg!' said Fox. Everyone was stunned.

'Are you crazy?' gasped Rabbit. 'I never heard of anything so disgusting in all my life.'

'As you like,' replied Fox. 'I told you it was a shocking thing. Go ahead, have it your way. It was just a thought.'

Nobody seemed to know how to respond. They seemed to be dazed. After waiting a bit Fox continued: 'What is worse, to lose a leg, or to lose your life? Now look at that leg; it's half off already. The steel trap cut through much of it. And the bone is broken for sure. Even if she did get out (which we all know she won't), she would never be able to use that leg again. So why not chew it off and set her free?'

Fox had said his piece. Everyone looked at Brother Beaver. As the husband of Betty, he would have to make the decision. It was clear that he wanted the best for his wife. But to tell them to chew off her leg? He wasn't ready for that.

'Just one more detail,' remarked Fox. 'If it's the leg, then we'd better do it soon, while Betty is still unconscious. That way she won't feel the pain. And she won't have to watch us doing it.'

There was silence. Nobody spoke. In the distance they could hear the roaring of the tractor. Presently Rabbit turned to Beaver and asked: 'Which is it? Her leg, or her life?'

Beaver fought with his feelings. He was close to tears. And then, in a voice that was just a bit shaky, he replied: 'Let's save her life.'

A few days later, when the man came back to the trap, he found it empty. There was only a leg in it and lots of blood splattered around. The beaver was gone.

'It fooled me!' he growled and stamped his foot on the ground. 'Tricked me, that's what it did!' The man mumbled to himself as he reset the trap. Then he walked away.

9

How Things Hang Together

At the side of the lake in the forest there was a rustling in the deep grass. Everyone heard it and kept low. By now the animals were taking no chances of being caught. That's why they were meeting in the deep grass. It would provide cover for them if the man came back.

And there was another reason for meeting beside the lake. It made it easier for Betty Beaver to attend. She didn't have to walk so far on her three legs.

The rustling noise came closer. And then they saw him. It was Fox. 'Sly as always,' Rabbit greeted Fox with a friendly smile. 'You're a bit late. But never mind. We were just talking about Betty. She has recovered remarkably well from the accident. And thanks to you, sly one, she is with us today. Alive and well!'

Fox was pleased. He was glad to see Betty doing so well, and he was happy that they had spoken well of him. He liked being praised.

'Good to see you, Betty,' he greeted Mrs Beaver. 'I just saw the man, and guess what? Ha, ha! He hasn't got four legs. He doesn't even have three legs. He walks on just two legs.'

'I suppose you want us to say that's funny,' replied Badger. 'But right now nothing about that man is funny. I hate him! That's right. I hate every part of him! Including his two stupid legs.'

Rabbit cleared his throat as if he was going to say something. But he didn't. He looked at Badger, and Badger turned to face him. They gazed deep into each other's eyes. Then Badger said: 'Sorry, Rabbit. Sorry, everybody. I shouldn't have said that.' Rabbit went over to Badger and put his paw gently on his shoulder.

'I know how you feel, Brother Badger. We all feel like that sometimes. Especially after all that the man has done to us. However, if anyone has a right to hate him, it is Betty Beaver.

'Betty, would you mind telling us how you feel about the man?'

'That's a bit difficult,' she replied. 'First, I want to thank all of you, and especially Fox, for saving my life. As you see, I'm doing nicely already on three legs. In a few weeks I'll run a race with any of you four-legged friends.

'As for the man, I think he is worse off than I am. Not because I have three legs and he has only two. I may be a cripple, but that man is blind. That's right, he's blind. And that's a lot worse.

'He can't see what he is doing to us animals. He can't see what he is doing to the birds. And to the trees. To everything that makes life good. He can't even see what he is doing to himself.

'Once his forest is gone and this is a car-park or a smoke-belching factory, there will be no birds here to sing for him. No birds to catch insects for him. No foxes to catch mice for him. There will be no . . .'

Everybody burst out laughing when she mentioned Fox catching mice. 'Hey, Foxy dear,' somebody shouted. 'You hear that? Do you eat mice with your chicken dinners?'

'Certainly,' replied Fox, not at all upset that they were making fun of him. 'I eat a hundred mice for every chicken I eat. If it weren't for me, that man would have his farm so overrun with mice that his cats would go berserk. Betty Beaver is absolutely right.'

Betty continued: 'The man is blind. Oh, he's got eyes all right, but he can't see. Once he cuts down his forest there will be less rain on his land. When rain clouds come along they'll just keep drifting over this area. They won't empty their water onto the land. It will get drier and drier. It might even become a desert.'

'Never heard that before,' said Beaver respectfully. 'I thought the rain fell evenly all over the earth. But perhaps I'm mistaken. I suppose you're right, Betty.'

'Of course she's right,' replied Rabbit. 'Have you ever worked out why it doesn't rain in the desert? Because there are no trees to put water in the air. And trees can't grow because it doesn't rain.

'It all hangs together, somehow. I think they call that ecology. Once the ecology is upset, you're in deep trouble. Betty is right; the man is blind. He can't see how he is hurting himself.'

'He should take a trip to a desert once,' suggested Badger. 'He'd learn fast.'

'Or to a rain forest,' countered Rabbit. 'Then he could work out the difference between a desert and a rain forest and how each of them got to be that way.'

'Thank you kindly,' said Betty Beaver. 'You helped me to make my little speech. There's only one more thing I'd·like to mention.

'Just as soon as all the trees are gone, good soil is going to wash away every time it rains, unless it is smothered under a car-park or factory. The roots that now hold the earth in place will be gone with the trees. There will be nothing at all, no leaves to protect and feed the soil.

'The best part of the soil is the topsoil. That's the top layer that produces the crops, like corn. But that good topsoil is all going to erode. First it gets washed into the rivers, and finally it gets carried out to the ocean.

'As hard as it is for us to imagine it now, one day this lovely area could become a desert. A barren place of nothing but sand and rocks, and a factory. No birds. No animals. No plants. Nothing but desert.'

Betty stopped. She had certainly given everyone a lot to think about. Everyone, that is, except the man. He was the one who should have heard this wonderful speech. But he was far away at this moment.

The man was planning a new way of using the monster tractor to lift the toppled tractor out of its grave. He was scheming how to get rid of the animals and birds. He was far away plotting how to rip out the forest in the shortest time.

Betty Beaver spoke again. 'I almost forgot to answer the question,' she apologised. 'Rabbit, you asked how I feel about the man and whether I hate him.

'Frankly, it is not easy to love someone who has made you lose your leg. I've had to struggle with that. But the more I think about it, the more I am convinced that the man is blind. And I cannot hate him for that.

'I think in another week or two, as I learn to get around on three legs, all the feelings of hate will be gone. Then I'll think only of one thing: How can we help to open the eyes of the man? It must be terrible to have eyes and not be able to see!' Betty stopped again.

Everyone waited because they could tell she was still not quite finished. At last she spoke once more and said:

'The man is blind and I am sorry for him. But he is not our enemy. He is foolish. He is stupid. Yes, and he is blind.

'He is not looking ahead to see what happens when the forests are gone. One day all this will be over. I hope we and our children will be friends with him again.'

Betty had hardly finished speaking when Starling came zooming through the air. She landed excitedly beside the group huddled together in the deep grass by the lake.

'What is it, Starling?' asked Rabbit. 'You seem to be excited.'

'It's the man!' she exclaimed. 'I watched him from way up high where he couldn't see me or shoot me. I followed him all the way to the forest. He's there right now. Close to the toppled tractor and the bird snares. He's got a double dose of mosquito repellent on him. He brought his gun and some more traps. And listen to this: he brought his dog.

'But that's not all. He brought a can with something white in it. From so far up I couldn't really tell what it is. It looks almost like grain, like little white kernels. He's got a spoon, and he's putting spoonfuls of this stuff here and there all over the forest.'

'He's mad! Absolutely out of his mind!' whispered Rabbit hoarsely. 'You all know what that stuff in the can is. Poison! He's putting poison all over the forest to kill us off so he can get on with cutting down the trees.'

'And then there's the dog,' responded Starling. 'He won't get me because I can fly away. But if I were you I'd start looking for my children at once.'

Starling had barely finished speaking when they heard one of Rabbit's own children crying. Mother Rabbit dashed away to find her little one. Moments later she came back holding the bunny with her front paws.

'What seems to be the problem, dear?' asked Mother Rabbit. 'Did you get lost? Were you frightened?'

'No,' replied the little one. 'I have a tummyache. It hurts so.' Mother Rabbit put her paw gently on her stomach and rubbed it. 'There, there, just lie still a bit, and it will all go away again. Perhaps you just ate something that doesn't agree with you.'

Baby Rabbit turned and twisted with the pain. Her whole body seemed to be aching. But then gradually she stopped whining and lay still. Father Rabbit smiled at his wife. She had the motherly touch that healed everything.

He asked the group to excuse them for the interruption they had caused. Then he explained that everything was all right now. Their baby Bunny had gone to sleep. They could now go on again with the meeting.

'Our baby is dead!' sobbed Mother Rabbit.

For a moment no one moved. They were so shocked. Father Rabbit took the little bunny into his arms. It was limp. There was no life in it.

'Poison!' someone said. 'She's been poisoned. She ate the stuff from the man's can.'

Rabbit didn't feel like continuing with the meeting. He just wanted to stay with his dead baby and sad wife. However, he knew that as the leader of the community he had other responsibilities.

A decision would have to be made. They would all have to act at once. Putting his arms lovingly around his wife and hugging his limp baby once more, he straightened up and said:

'Listen, everybody, listen carefully. First, all of you, get to your families. Warn your children not to touch those white kernels. Tell them what it will do to them. Tell them what happened to our baby.

'Second, watch out for the traps and the dog.

And birds, stay away from those snares. We'll meet again here, on the same spot, as soon as the moon is up.

'We have little time left. And as you know, we have few ideas on how to save our forest home. Run along now. Be careful. See you all when the moon is up.'

10

In Deep Trouble

Later that evening Rabbit watched beside the lake. One after the other, his friends and neighbours came sneaking along their familiar paths back to the meeting place in the deep grass. At last they were all assembled – except Fox. He was usually late. Rabbit suggested they wait for him.

There were no clouds in the sky. The moon was round and full. Somebody reminded them of the good times they used to have in the forest when there was a full moon and before all this trouble had begun. Starling was confident the good times would return again.

'Won't that be wonderful!' replied Rabbit. 'We'll celebrate for a week.'

'And invite the man to celebrate with us,' added Betty Beaver.

'Without his gun and dog,' chuckled Fox, as he stepped through the deep grass. He had been hiding there for the last few minutes listening to their conversation.

'And without traps, tractors, snares, and poison,' added Rabbit. 'So let's start the meeting. Foxy, our sly friend, is here at last.'

At first they talked about how well everything had gone in the beginning. How successfully Badger had toppled the tractor. How Operation Sting had almost driven the man wild. How gloriously funny Operation Stink had been. Skunky had sent that man home perfumed for life and almost naked. Yes, those had been good days.

But then came the not-so-good days. When Operation Feathers, for example, was an almost complete disaster. When phase two of Operation Sting had failed because the man had used mosquito repellent lotion.

And then there were the casualties. Dead mosquitoes and birds. The dead bunny rabbit. There was the loss of Betty's leg, and a lot more. The worst of it was that the man was now using everything he had to hurt them – gun, snares, traps, poison, and even the dog.

Finally Rabbit said: 'We're in deep trouble. If we hadn't decided long ago not to move, I'd suggest we get out of here now. What do you say?'

'We can't move now,' replied Betty Beaver. 'There's no other forest nearby. I'm still hoping we can open the eyes of the man. He'll see that we are not his enemies but his friends.'

'That's exactly how I feel,' added Brother Beaver in support of his wife. 'It's too late now to move. We're all too much involved in this. We've got to see it through to the end. If we're going to live with ourselves later, we can't quit now.'

'And don't forget what I told you more than once,' added Fox. 'There is no other place to go to. There is no other forest nearby just waiting for us. This is our home. Our *only* home.'

'Very well, then,' said Rabbit. 'Nobody has changed his mind. So we're staying. Okay. Then what do you suggest we do now?'

'Operation Water, Operation Water,' chimed everyone at the same time. 'Let's sock it to him with a splash!' somebody shouted. 'Let's see whether the man can swim,' somebody laughed with a sneer.

'Let's see what he'll do when he gets his feet wet! Let's drown his stupid tractor. Let him get a boat!'

Everybody had something to say. Rabbit was certain they were all agreed on Operation Water. This was their last resort. So turning to Beaver he said: 'You hear what they say. Are you up to it? Betty, will you manage on three legs? And are you still sure you're prepared to give up your home for this cause? You have already made a big sacrifice.'

The beavers looked at each other, but only for a moment. 'Just tell us when,' replied Brother Beaver.

'Just tell us when and we'll do it,' agreed Betty. 'But the rest of you had better look out for yourselves and your families when that water starts coming. Have you thought about what's going to happen to your homes? When we pull the plug, when we break the dam, we will be safe but you will get wet.'

For a moment that took some of them by surprise. They had only thought about flooding the man's land. They hadn't realised that the whole forest and their own homes would also be flooded.

But Fox came to the rescue again. He explained which part of the forest was lowland and which part was high ground. All they had to do was make sure they and their children scrambled quickly to the higher ground before Operation Water began.

It turned out to be a long meeting. In the end everyone was satisfied that Operation Water was finally going to do it. It would bring the man to his senses. Or, as Betty Beaver had said so well, it would open his eyes.

In the end the eyes of the man actually were opened. Not by Operation Water, however, but by something quite different. Something so strange that the animals and birds at first had trouble believing and understanding it. For now, however, everyone knew what to do.

As usual, Rabbit gave the signal. Within an hour the land was completely under water. People from the town came out to see it and to take pictures. The animals watched from their higher ground.

Starling was high in the sky getting a good view of the whole situation. Every now and then she flew back, made a nosedive down to Rabbit's command post, and gave him an up-to-the-minute report.

The water continued to pour out of the lake, she said. And there was still lots of water left to run out. She said the beavers were okay. People had started to talk about the flood on the radio. Then she was off.

Starling was a good observer and accurate reporter. When she came back again with more information, she said she had seen the TV people making videos of the flood for the evening news.

Fire engines were gathering along the edge of the water. However, there was nothing that anyone could do about stopping the water from coming.

Off she went for the nineteenth time and came back telling Rabbit that he had given the signal at exactly the right time. The man had left his farm and was halfway between his home and the forest when the water came. It had come so fast that he couldn't turn around, and he couldn't go on to the higher ground either. He was trapped.

His monster tractor was stuck so deep in the mud and water, she was sure it would be many days before they could get it out again. And the man's other tractor, the one Badger had toppled, was completely under water. She couldn't see it at all.

Somewhere along the road the fire service was attempting to unload a boat, she said. Starling supposed it was for rescuing the man from the tractor.

The animals and birds were thrilled with all that was happening. It certainly was also exciting for the farmer. Not only for him but for a lot of people in the area. By supper-time everybody in town knew what had happened as well.

By the next morning the mayor, the police, and the news media wanted to know what had happened. And even more than that, they wanted to know *why* it had happened.

The only one who could answer that question was the farmer. The man who owned the land and the lake. He had been stuck on his tractor until midnight, so he was not available for comment in the evening. However, the firemen had rescued him with the boat. Now everyone wanted to hear what he might have to say.

After so much news Starling was suddenly able to report little more. In the morning everything was quiet in town. The man's tractor was still out in the mud and water. The toppled tractor was still covered with water. But the man himself could not be seen anywhere.

11

The Sly Spy Fox

Rabbit didn't like it. In fact, none of the animals liked this kind of silence. Always after an attack the man had come back to get even with them. But not this time.

What was he up to? Where was he? Why didn't he do anything? Was he perhaps planning a major sneak attack on them? Was he getting more help from the people in town? They waited all day for some new development, but nothing happened.

As soon as it was dark Rabbit called another meeting. 'What's up?' he asked. 'Why isn't there any action? Why doesn't the man show himself?'

Somebody suggested that perhaps he had drowned. Everybody knew that wasn't true. 'Perhaps he decided to give up,' said somebody else. But the others all thought that was just wishful thinking.

Rabbit cleared his throat the way he often did when he had something important to say. 'This news blackout is making us all nervous,' he began. 'We simply have to know what is going on.

'Foxy,' he continued, motioning to Fox to come closer. 'Foxy, this is your chance to show us how clever you really are. We appoint you to go and investigate. Find out all you can and bring us a report as quickly as possible.'

Fox didn't even look a bit surprised. Night prowling was nothing new to him. Snooping around in strange places didn't frighten him in the least. And he was a good actor, so even if he was surprised he wouldn't show it.

'Yes, of course,' Fox replied in a matter-of-fact way. 'I'll go and spy for you. See you soon.'

Rabbit called after him to be careful, but he was already gone. Everyone was tired from the long day's excitement, especially the suspense of waiting. When Rabbit suggested they all had best get some sleep, they were glad for that.

It must have been about midnight when the animals heard a scratching noise and a muffled yelp. Then they heard a familiar voice saying, 'I'm back. Where are you?'

It was Fox. In no time at all everybody awoke,

came out of the grass and bushes, and crowded around Fox. They all wanted to hear what he had to say.

'How was it? Did you see anybody?' asked Badger.

'Did you see the man? Where is he? What's he up to now?' asked Rabbit eagerly.

'Were you in danger? Did you go to the farm? Did you run into the dog?' asked Skunk.

But Fox wouldn't say a word. He just sat down, stretched his legs, and replied. 'Not so fast, not so fast. That's a lot of questions at once.'

'Well, come now,' demanded Rabbit good-naturedly. 'We're glad to see you safely back. But now give us your report. Please.'

'Yes, yes,' replied Fox. 'Just give me time to catch my breath. Don't you realise how far I've travelled while you slept? Have you any idea what dangers I have been in while you were all safe? Have you any notion how hard I've worked while you were as lazy as a bug in a rug?'

Fox stretched and yawned. 'Don't mind my teasing you a bit,' he said in good spirits. 'But seriously, I am hungry and thirsty. Nobody has offered me food since I came back. Isn't there anything to drink around here? I'm thirsty.'

'Sorry,' replied Rabbit. 'We're pushing you too hard. Will somebody get Foxy something to drink? Betty, could you get him something to eat?'

'But you will tell us tonight yet, won't you?' And then, looking Fox straight in the eye, Rabbit continued in a serious tone of voice: 'You do have something to tell us, don't you? I hope you haven't just been chasing chickens again.'

Fox sat back and yawned. He enjoyed being the centre of attention. If he could draw it out, so much the better. He smiled when he saw their curiosity and how nice they all were to him.

'Well,' demanded Rabbit again. 'Do you have something to tell us?'

'Oh yes,' replied Fox, 'I most certainly do! And when you hear it you'll flip. I'll probably have to tell it to you three times before you believe me.' He stretched again, yawned, and pretended to be sleepy.

There was nothing anybody could do. Fox was Fox and that was that. When he was ready to talk, he would talk. They knew that begging wouldn't help. So they just waited. They brought him food and drink. They smiled at him and were as nice to him as possible.

All of a sudden Fox jumped up, stood in the middle of the circle of animals and birds, and let out a squeal that sounded just a bit weird. He began to laugh. He laughed so heartily that Rabbit wasn't the only one who began to wonder whether he had lost a few of his marbles. But it was just an act. A good act really, if they had known what Foxy knew.

Then just as suddenly as he had started laughing, he stopped, got sober, and began to talk.

He talked for over an hour. He had so much to say. Everybody listened intently. It was an incredible story.

It had all started with the flood. People had begun to ask questions: Where did the water come from? Why did the lake flood?

The police had brought the man in for questioning. At first he didn't want to say much. But when the mayor of the town pointed out the damage the water had done to some of the houses, he began to talk.

At the town council they reported that fortunately no lives had been lost. But they still didn't know why the dam had broken and flooded the land. Couldn't the farmer give them any clues at all?

'The beavers did it,' replied the farmer. 'It's as simple as that. The beavers did it.'

'They broke their own dam?' asked the mayor with great surprise. 'Now why in the world would a beaver do that? Never heard of such a thing! As far as I know, beavers build dams; they don't break them.'

'Are you quite sure about that?' asked one of the townspeople. 'And if you are, do you have an explanation for such strange behaviour?'

The man didn't want to tell them everything, but

he was getting in deeper all the time. There was no way out now that they had uncovered this much. So he told them about Betty Beaver's leg. He thought maybe that had made the beavers angry. To get even with him, they had broken the dam and flooded his land.

'Say that again,' asked a lady in the audience. 'Did I hear you say that a beaver lost a leg? I happen to represent a society which fights cruelty to animals. I'd be interested in hearing more about this. How did the beaver lose its leg?'

12

The Man in the Hot Seat

The man began to squirm and to sweat. By now they were really on to him. It was worse than Operation Sting. There seems to be nothing you can spray on your skin to keep people off your back the way you keep mosquitoes away. So he had to tell them about the steel traps.

Before long he had to admit to setting nets and snares for the birds. They heard about the gun and the dog. But the man wasn't stupid, and he knew his rights. He knew that these people could give him a rough time, but that was all.

They couldn't punish him or stop him. He had a permit to trap animals he claimed were damaging his property. There was no law against dogs. He had a gun licence. And he had been on his own land.

But he knew there was a law against poison. That's why he tried so hard to keep that secret. In his mind he was repeating to himself: 'They mustn't find out about the poison. They mustn't find out about the poison.'

'Did you say something just now?' asked the mayor. 'I don't think we quite heard you.'

The man was surprised by the question. He opened his mouth as if he wanted to speak, but nothing came out. He didn't say anything.

His hands trembled. His face was pale. At last he stammered. 'No, I wasn't saying anything. Nothing, really.'

'But why are you so nervous?' asked one of the firemen. 'You seem to be in worse shape now than when we rescued you from your drowning tractor at midnight.'

'Tell us about that,' the mayor urged the fireman. 'Just what happened last night when you went out there with the boat to save the farmer?'

The fireman reported that there wasn't much to tell. It was all quite simple. They had gone out to the tractor to pick up the stranded man and some of the things he had on the tractor with him. That was all.

'What sort of things did you pick up from the tractor?' asked a lady.

'Nothing much,' replied the fireman. 'Just the snares and traps, the net and logging chain, the gun, of course. And a can of poison.'

When he said poison, the farmer almost fell off his chair. 'Poison!' repeated the lady. 'Did I hear you right? Did you say poison?'

'Why yes,' replied the fireman. 'There was a can of poison. We picked that up, too, because we didn't want the water to get to it. You know, ma'am, what might happen then. I don't need to explain that.

'But none of the poison got into the water. You can be sure of that. Nobody needs to be afraid. The water out there and in this town is clean and safe.'

Well, that did it. The secret was no longer a secret. 'From where I was hiding and watching the whole thing,' said Fox, 'I was almost sorry for the man.

'The mayor asked more questions. And when the mayor stopped, the people picked up where he had left off. And the media people probed into every detail. The poor man had to tell everything. And the people were furious.'

'You could have poisoned our cats and dogs,' shouted one man. 'Our pets often go out into the woods.'

'And our children,' snapped another. 'They pick wild berries in the forest.'

In the end they threw the book at him. They

let him know that what he had done had been extremely careless. And very dangerous.

Some suggested arresting the farmer and bringing him to trial. Others thought that if he was sorry and promised never to do anything like that again, they should let him go.

Fox was playing all this back to the animals and birds so vividly that they felt as though they had been there themselves. He did it so well that in their minds they could almost see and hear the people. Foxy, the sly one, surely was a good reporter. He had done them all a valuable service.

When at last he stopped, they thought he was finished. But he had only paused for breath. There was more.

'Hold it, don't go away yet,' said Fox. 'that's only the first part of the story. I told you it would knock you down. You haven't heard the last part yet.'

Rabbit motioned for everyone to sit down again. 'Proceed, Fox,' he requested. 'If there is more good news, we surely want to hear it.'

Fox did enjoy playing it to them. All eyes were on him. This was great. That's how he liked it. They'd never forget this night, he was sure. And whenever they would talk about it in years to come, perhaps to their children and grandchildren, they would say, 'Fox did it! Our own Fox did it!'

At last he stopped fantasising and said: 'I'll make this short.' He waited a bit before starting again and was just a little bit disappointed that they all didn't protest and say, No, don't make it short. Make it as long as the first part.

But then he looked at the moon and saw how late it was. He looked into their faces and saw how tired they were. So he continued.

He told them of some men at the meeting who said they represented an organisation called Great Programme. It had that name because they wanted to protect the environment, the ecology, to keep the world healthy and green, and to stop the violence.

'They talked about attempting to halt nuclear tests. They said even underground atomic explosions were bad for all of us. They told of Great Programme people going up in balloons to ground zero, right over the target, to stop atomic blasts. They want to protect the air from pollution.

'They work extra hard to protect the water. They are always testing rivers and lakes as well as the oceans. They try to stop the dumping of toxic wastes, or poison, into the water.

'They go around and protest and march. In Parliament they lobby against people who ruin our world. They demonstrate and publish all kinds of stuff. He said hundreds and thousands of people were joining them in peaceful demonstrations.

'Somebody asked them what they called themselves, other than by their name, Great Programme. Their leader replied that they were sometimes called ecological activists.

'If you ask me,' Fox continued, 'I didn't understand half of what he said. Sometimes I thought the man was nuts. But I did understand when he said that the Great Programme people believe the earth is not ours to do with as we please. It belongs to our children and grandchildren. I liked that.'

On and on Fox went, talking about these people and their concern for the environment. For plants and soil, for water and air, fish and birds. And, of course, for the animals.

And then Fox told them how all of a sudden the Great Programme speaker had taken three steps forward to where the man was sitting. He pointed his finger straight at him. He looked him right in the eye.

Then in a voice that was almost a whisper he said: 'You are destroying the universe! You are upsetting the ecological balance! You are tampering with the environment!'

Had the man shouted those words they would not have been nearly as effective as when he said them in his low and even tone. Fox said it was so quiet in the room you could have heard a pin drop.

He went on: 'The man just sat there. Squashed. He had slumped down in his chair and looked more miserable than a rabbit just before he's turned into rabbit stew.'

'Did you say rabbit stew?' asked Rabbit. 'That's

not funny. But because you did all of us an outstanding service tonight, I'll overlook that crude remark. Thank you, Foxy, for your detailed report. Are there any questions?'

'I would be interested in knowing how our friend Fox got into the village and into the town hall where all this is supposed to have happened. How come he wasn't seen by anyone?' asked Badger.

Fox smiled his best foxy smile. Then he replied: 'That's my secret. I guess that's why you call me the sly one. If you're not a fox yourself, forget it. You'd never learn the trick, and you wouldn't even understand it if I told you.

'Why, most of you couldn't even get into a chicken coop and steal a chicken without getting caught. We foxes do that when we're still babies.'

Rabbit wanted to tell Fox that he was bragging. But he had already given him a bit of a scolding before, about the rabbit stew, so he let it go. He didn't want to annoy Fox.

Instead he said, 'Fox, you have been a great help to us. Thank you.'

13

The Great Shalom

Rabbit continued: 'And thank you all who contributed so much to saving our forest home.

'Thank you, Badger, for your successful Operation Topple. Thank you, mosquitoes, for your courageous and equally successful Operation Sting. And thank you, Skunky, for the magnificent performance of Operation Stink.

'Thank you, Madam Starling and all your birds, for Operation Feathers. It wasn't your fault that it wasn't a hundred percent successful. Who could have known that the man would come with a gun and start shooting you out of the air? Sorry you lost some of your friends.

'And thank you, Brother and Betty Beaver, for

Operation Water. That finally turned things around for us. Sorry for you too, Betty, that it cost you your leg.'

At that point Badger jumped up and asked for permission to say a few words.

'I speak for everyone,' he began, 'when I say, thank you, Rabbit. Without you as our leader we never would have got where we are today. And you, too, made a sacrifice. Sorry about your baby.'

He sat down. Everyone applauded. Mother Rabbit wiped a tear from her eye. Rabbit made a slight bow.

He thanked them and asked, 'Where do we go from here? What is our next move? The woods are secure. Our forest home has been saved. And you will agree that the experience of the last days has brought us all closer together.'

'There is one more thing we need to do as a group,' began Betty Beaver. 'We need to put our heads together and plan a strategy for making peace with the man. He needs us especially at this time when everyone is down on him. He needs to know that we are his friends.

'Let me say it once more: I think the man is blind. Or rather, he was blind. Now his eyes are opened. So now is the time for us to let him know how we feel about him. He needs to know that we care for him.'

It was a wonderful little speech. Everyone liked

it. There was a long applause. The animals smiled at each other. There was a great feeling of warm friendship among them. If the man could be included in this, too, then they all would be happy and satisfied.

Rabbit rose to say something. 'Betty Beaver has spoken for all of us,' he began. 'Her words came from her heart, and our hearts said yes to all of them. The best and most fitting way to celebrate our victory is to make peace with the man. In our hearts we already have peace with him, but he doesn't know that yet.

'I am sure he, too, wishes for harmony and happiness to return to our community. A community in which there is room for all of us birds and animals as well as the man.

'It's too late now to work out the details of the strategy. But by now we all know what strategy means. We know how to work at it. And we know how important a good plan is. We are too tired now and need to get some rest. But first thing tomorrow morning, let's all meet here again and plan the Great Shalom.'

'The Great Shalom?' asked Skunky. 'What's that?'

'Shalom means peace,' explained Rabbit. 'The biggest and best peace of all. Shalom includes happiness, love, contentment, health, harmony, and everything good. So please all come back here tomorrow morning. It'll be our best meeting of all. The meeting for planning the Great Shalom.'

'The Great Shalom,' mused Skunky thoughtfully to himself. 'The Great Shalom! I think that's something for me to work on, too.'

The moon drifted silently over the forest. There wasn't a cloud in the sky. All the animals and birds were asleep at last. They were dreaming of tomorrow. Dreaming about their happiest meeting of all. The strategy meeting for planning the Great Shalom.

If you have enjoyed this story, here are some other *Tiger* books you might like to read.

Greenlands Adventure
Cathie Bartlam

Sal and her class spend half-term week at Greenlands adventure camp. Sal loves all the activities – canoeing, raft-building, assault courses – and is determined that her gang will be best. She cannot understand why Tag is different. Then a night adventure goes wrong and Sal realises she needs help too.

Another story about the characters in *Tricky Business*.

Fox in the Den
Geraldine Witcher

Sarah finds an abandoned puppy in the woods and takes it back to the den to look after it. But it is not a puppy – it is a fox cub and harder to care for. She tries to keep it secret and Kit helps her. Then the cub becomes ill and they have to find help. Will they lose the cub? Who killed the mother fox? Sarah and her friends follow trails to find the truth.

Another story about the characters in *Runaway in the Den*.

A Rosette for Helen
Doreen Bairstow
Jo and Clare have been looking forward to the pony holiday week at the local riding stables. But they are jealous of Helen, who is a better rider, and refuse to be friends with her. They plan to show her up but the plan goes disastrously wrong and has results none of them could foresee.

Dancing Feet
Veronica Heley
Pippa loves dancing and her weekly class is a highlight of her life. But when it clashes with her brother Tom's cricket coaching, she has to give up the class. Tom seems to be good at everything. Pippa feels good at nothing – except dancing – and her dancing teacher is keen to give her an opportunity to shine. Will Pippa get into the pantomime?